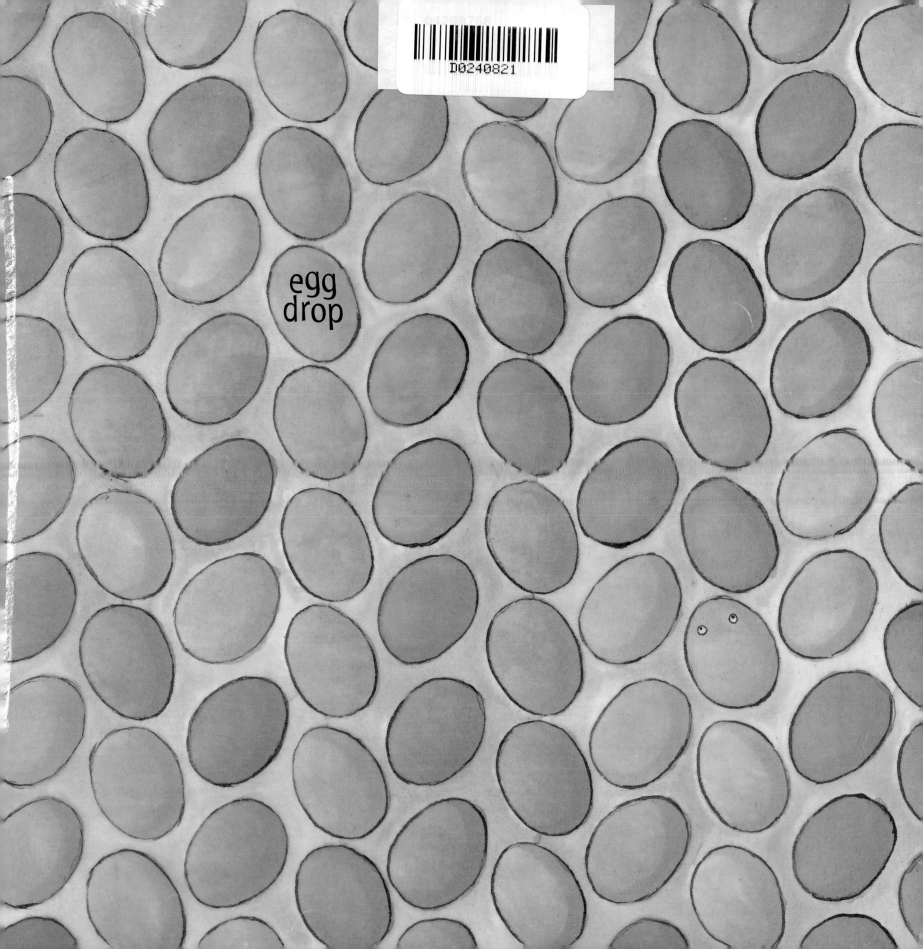

egg
drop

D0240821

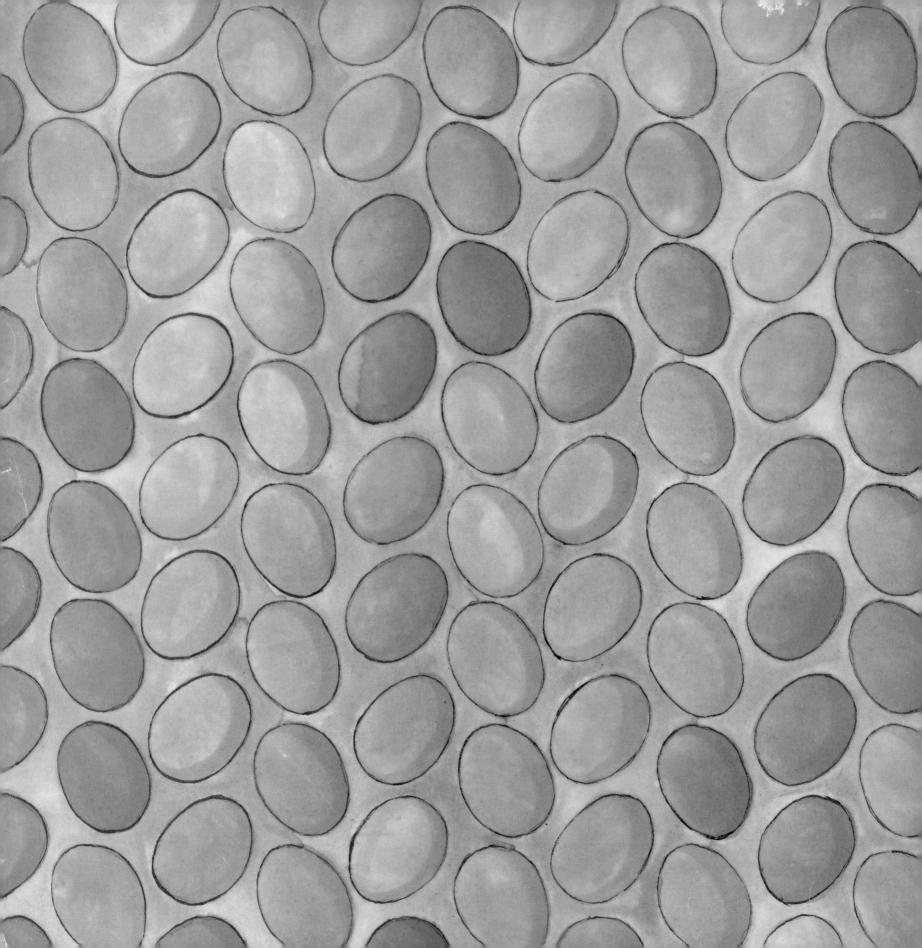

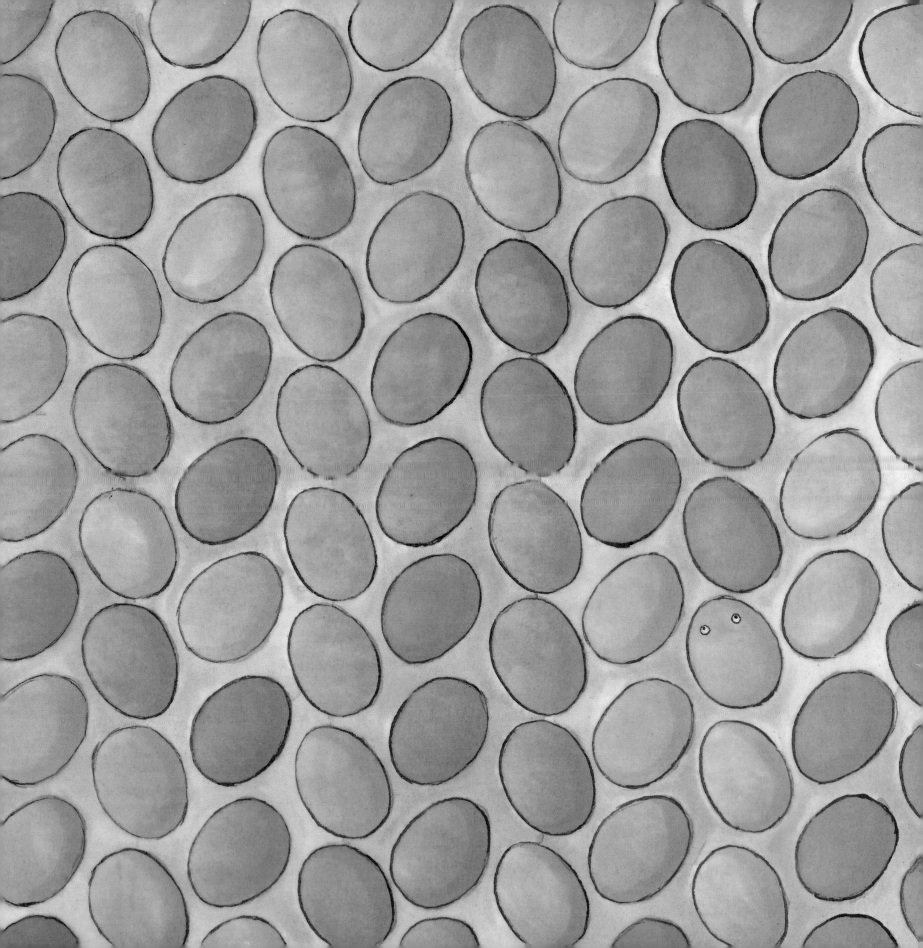

To Tony

BRENT LIBRARIES

04268758	
PETERS	19-Dec-07
£5.99	KIN

egg
drop

Mini Grey

RED FOX

The Egg was young.
It didn't know much.
We tried to tell it,
but of course it didn't listen.

If only it had waited.

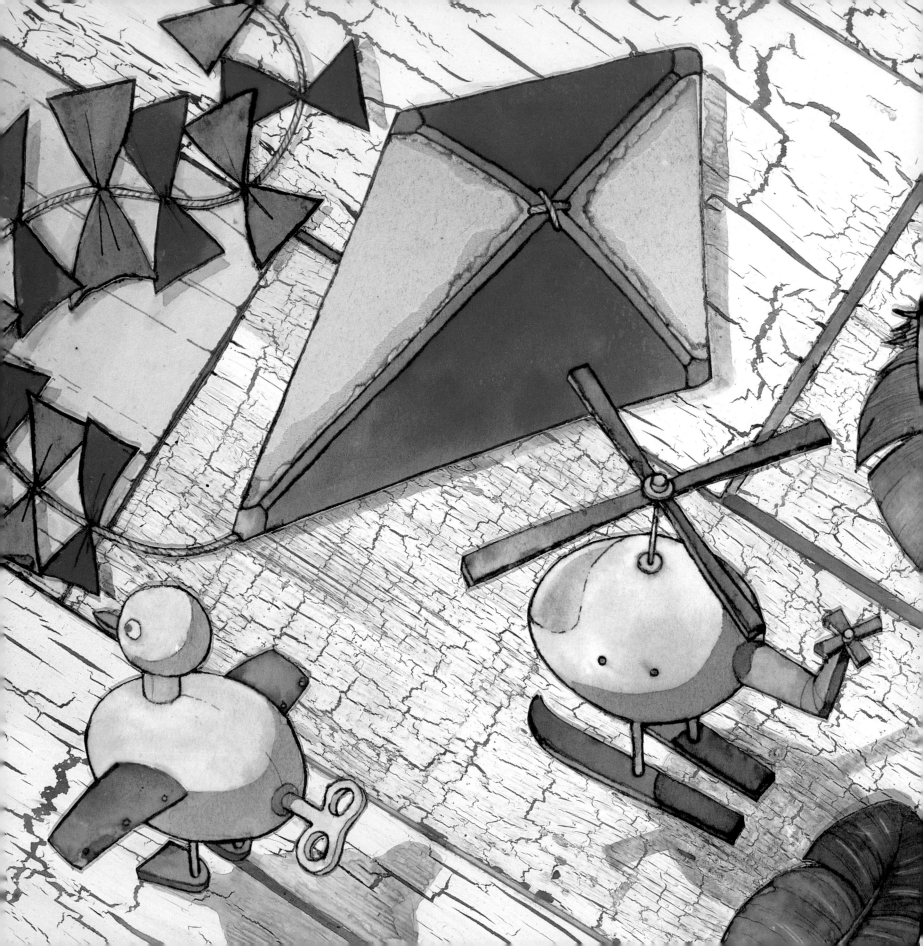

Here is the story of the egg that wanted to fly.

The Egg had always loved looking up,
seeing birds and balloons,
aeroplanes and insects,
helicopters and bats and clouds.

The Egg wanted to fly with them.
It dreamed of ways to fly.

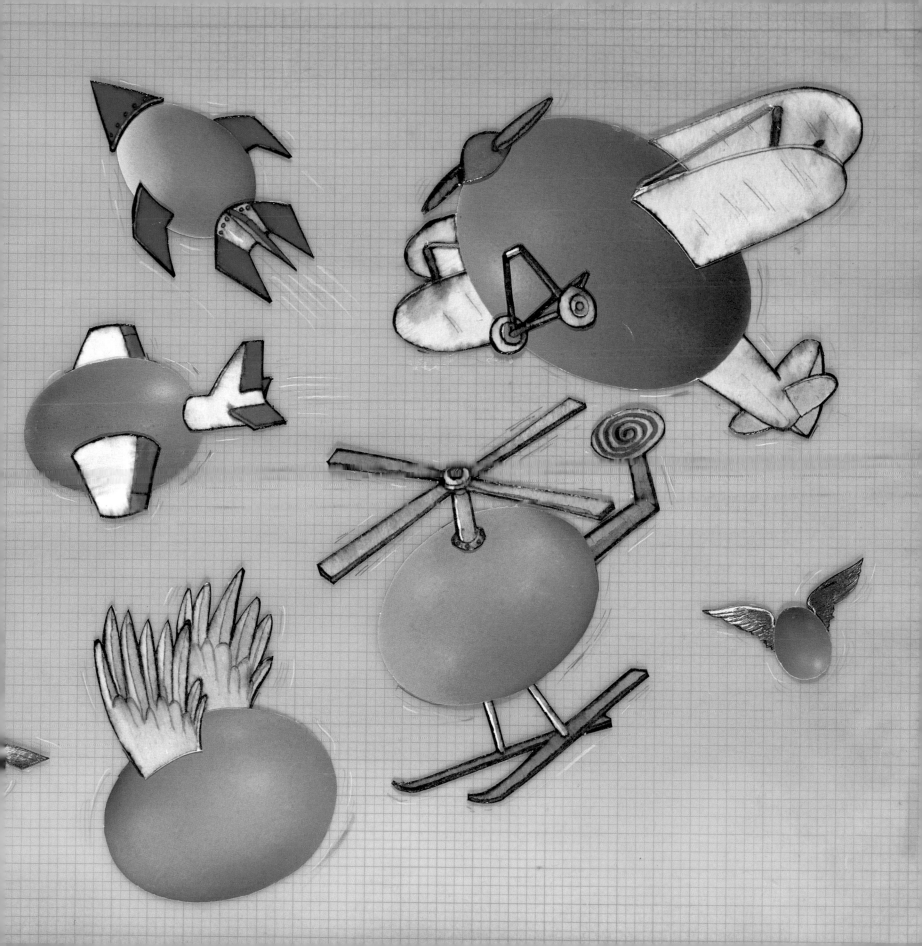

But the Egg was young.
It didn't know much about flying
(and it didn't know anything
about aerodynamics
or Bernoulli's Principle).

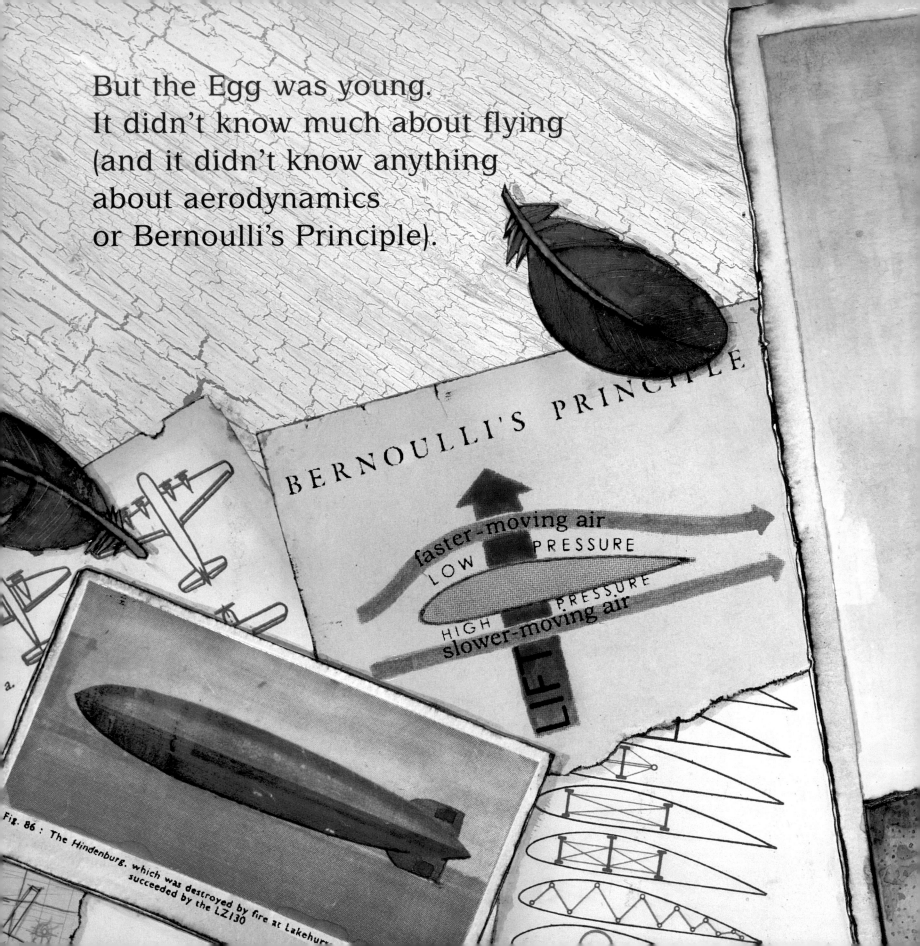

BERNOULLI'S PRINCIPLE

faster-moving air
LOW PRESSURE
HIGH PRESSURE
slower-moving air
LIFT

Fig. 86 : The Hindenburg, which was destroyed by fire at Lakehurst
succeeded by the LZ130

It just knew that it
had to get up high.

There was
a very tall tower
made of bricks
on a hill.
Inside there were
583 stone steps.

AN OF THE TOWE

The Egg climbed
to the top.

The Egg was in the clouds.
A bird flew past.
The Egg squeezed its eyes shut.
It drew a deep breath.
It took a step into space.

There was an enormous egg rush.

The Egg opened its eyes and saw
friends in the air, felt sky blasting past.

"Whee!" it cried. "I am flying!"

But the Egg
was not flying.

It was falling.

It took us a while to clear up the mess.

We tried to put the Egg back together again,

sewing

chewing gum

nails

and

screws

tomato soup

but nothing really worked and shells don't heal.

The Egg was young.
It didn't listen.
If only it had waited.

FARM NEWS

EGG DROP!

THE TRAGIC end of a local egg as discovered yesterday at the ase of the Very Tall Tower. The gg was found to be irreparably roken and rapidly losing albumen. Emergency services were called immediately by local poultry but all attempts at resuscitation failed. When questioned about the egg's unlucky demise, a witness reportedly commented: "The egg was young. It didn't listen. If only it had waited." When pressed to comment further the witness merely shrugged its wings and waddled slowly away. Police have asserted that there is no suspicion of fowl play.

TOO YOUNG....the egg that wanted to fly

For further information about how to make good use of broken eggs turn to our Cookery Section on page 23. Recipes in our special feature include *Oeufs en Cocotte* and *Egg Pie*, but we also preview extracts from *Cooking Eggs for Invalids*, a new book by Celia

Luckily, the Egg was not wasted.

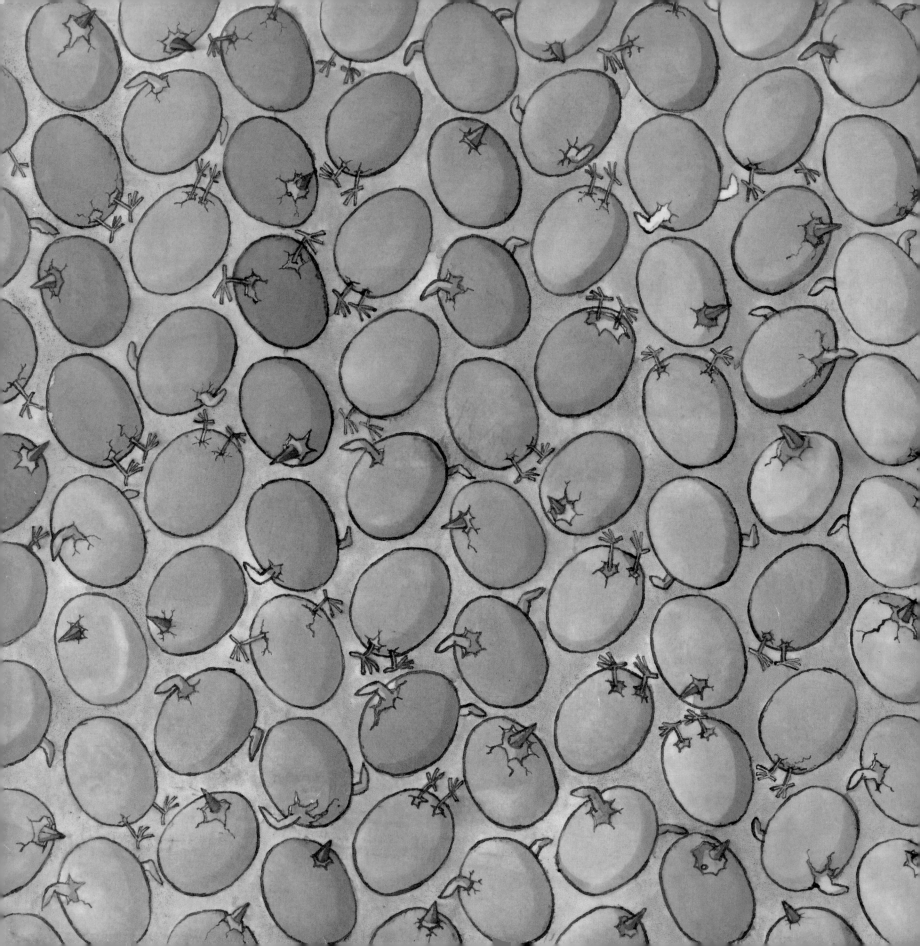

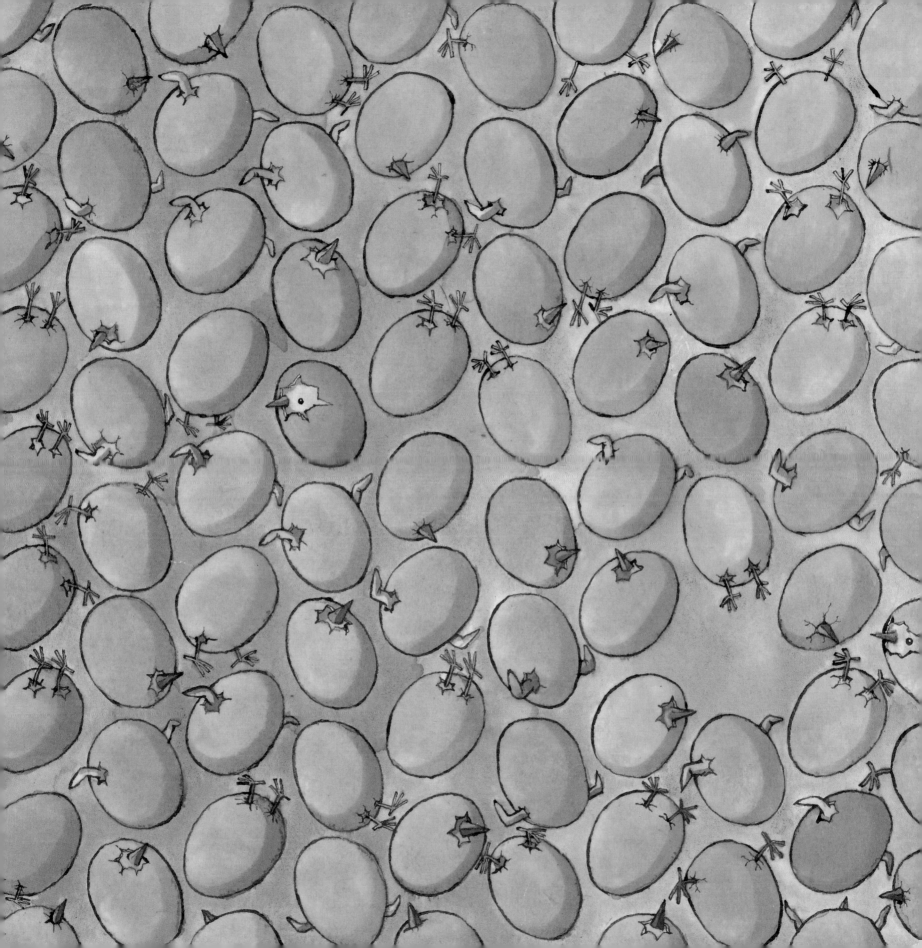

A RED FOX BOOK
978 0 099 43203 6

First published in Great Britain by Jonathan Cape,
an imprint of Random House Children's Books

Jonathan Cape edition published 2002
Red Fox edition published 2003

7 9 10 8 6

Copyright © Mini Grey, 2002

The right of Mini Grey to be identified as the author and illustrator of this
work has been asserted in accordance with the Copyright, Designs and Patents Act 1988

All rights reserved. No part of this publication may be reproduced,
stored in a retrieval system, or transmitted in any form or by any means,
electronic, mechanical, photocopying, recording or otherwise,
without the prior permission of the publishers.

Red Fox Books are published by Random House Children's Books,
61–63 Uxbridge Road, London W5 5SA,
A Random House Group Company
Addresses for companies within The Random House
Group Limited can be found
at: www.randomhouse.co.uk/offices.htm

THE RANDOM HOUSE GROUP Limited Reg. No. 954009
www.rbooks.co.uk

A CIP catalogue record for this book is available from the British Library.

Printed in Singapore by Tien Wah Press [PTE] Ltd